1ST OF FEB, BORN

POEMS , CREATIVE ASSENCE OF DIVINE

AYAANSH RITURAJ

Copyright © Ayaansh Rituraj
All Rights Reserved.

This book has been published with all efforts taken to make the material error-free after the consent of the author. However, the author and the publisher do not assume and hereby disclaim any liability to any party for any loss, damage, or disruption caused by errors or omissions, whether such errors or omissions result from negligence, accident, or any other cause.

While every effort has been made to avoid any mistake or omission, this publication is being sold on the condition and understanding that neither the author nor the publishers or printers would be liable in any manner to any person by reason of any mistake or omission in this publication or for any action taken or omitted to be taken or advice rendered or accepted on the basis of this work. For any defect in printing or binding the publishers will be liable only to replace the defective copy by another copy of this work then available.

I here begin with my fresh epitome of craziness of thinking, where we need to think ,think and re- think that's biggest gift which we as human being has recieved .

I as poet will not convey more but as poem will really gratify you in nameshake of happiness .

Willingly writing poem really fascinates me and makes sense of present .

'A fascinating journey gives you a chance to create present.....'

'TRY NOT TO DEFINE FUTURE'

....

Contents

Foreword

Well in piece of Literature in our Classic school text books we need not to read it.

but as demand and certain rules created by head majesty of publisher I need to write .

basically about poems and many more stuffs which give better finishing.

enjoying poems means feel .

Emotion made reader more and more like joking which more reactify and glory your character .

I find little more interesting to defile beauty in a character of nature because thats means of communication..

LAUGHING ! thats PLEASANT MOMENT ....

Preface

So this poetry is all about instances created around nature .

literally saying Book doesn't give or create that aura in your attitude to read but it really transforms, frankly saying you will not enjoy at that point of time .

to stress this out , I started saying poetry.

My poetry is phychological music for beautiful mind .

Poems like 'Atheist Interpreter' , 'Dark Days' and my very favourite

'Rudest Proposal' are collection of my poetry .

I usually write poetry for creation and deep awake myself , I don't want to counter attack, but what to do, for me thats a only medium ....

NOW DON'T WASTE YOUR TIME .

" EXPLORE ME "

quick.....

Introduction

Risking my inner joy in front of someone.........

I want to share my experience more but believe me poems are memorable journey for me .

My name is Ayaansh Rituraj my original name is Rituraj given by my beloved Parents .

but when it comes what can you do on your pace , you really need to create your own devastating journey .

from every family situation there is time to escape I am one of them .

I am studying with learning attitude,frankly thats gives me ideas of writing poems . I live in varanasi .

"I don't have Introduction I am creating it"

"MAD BOND "

1. Poem - Atheist Interpreter

Flower is a versatility

which covers round

To protect , to know more

absent waterbodies

where they fall ,where I grow

starving to save them

to grow in new prose

"In outer covering and dare they fell in free new fall "

"New day to Last day"

"Same pond to Same destiny"

"Same time to same define"

"Same vibe to Same life"

"In cool shine dimensions new vine"

"New Era"

"New Life Greif"

I am Alive !

a lot discriminate

course of design beauty

connecting to mighty powers

in serve cave " I am Atheist "

I am divine vine

known as "INTERPRETER "

coury allow me to fall

its time to understand a madness of "Mighty"

glory decides destiny

glory satire in a glory mood

diversify I reach

"DIVINE"understand Atheist...

I portray ,my life. my satire . and my cvontroversy

how I fall ,how I breathe ..

Mighty! are you Insane

malicious existence beauty

reached in dilemma

MY CONDOLENCES!!

my image signifies, "Mighty Laugh"!

existence diverting new bond

beauty console the "FLOWERS" charm.

....

2. Poem - Deep Awaken

Legends have faith, Majesty have tired

myths lasts long to entertain

couring have quest. legends are awaken

powerful are watching

myths is diverting

curious cubic diagonose having faith

faith diverts the majesty

courtesy is dissolving

parents are buying myths

crowding in long hours

feeling alone in night hours

creating alone sky

encounter parents charm truly

courage awaken under legends

legends are drowning

verily beneith the sky

sky console the fatters fry

loudy time asking for spirit

Legends Lost, Legends Forget, Legends Notch

legends says .....

when you cry for hours

wipe your tears

remember the past

which Deep "Awakens" you .

....

3. Poem - Rudest Proposal

I was curious to know my vision

whom I approach every moment

a cracking mood to indegenous craze

lower pitch of voice always affectionate me

I ought to understand my assence

new moon ! I was delighted

I know to whom I am talking

though to whom I am approaching

caring the determination unorganise

I always diversify myself as a protagonist

I was not authorised but frightened to get notice

proposal was respectful, answer was rudest

I was unaware of atheist behavior

talking to my harness friend in destroyer alived

I was amazed with treatment ,she pursued in front of me

I decided never try to define in front of her

it slighted me , I was obdient in my own way

happy company in suddened moon

fastened nights in daring mare

I was instinctual but staedy to commit fragile behaviour

I was awake graveyard from now

today I always be quite in front of her

never release my emotive emotions till she ask me

believing in vision of bilindness nature

but still affectionate of "I" matters !

....

4. Poem - Massacre Beauty

Baby crying in guard of mother shell

some got awake , some got slept

next sprouty day , he got himself

he was kid very dark, very cliche

some got offend, some got vary attack

he was scare

assence of maiden affair

I was alive sitting there

round deck roof

enjoying hot shaded shadow

he said...

O! mighty brother sitting in blasting roof

are you mad ? questioned vary kid

verily ! I was sitting under roof dear.

It is darky ,questioned smartly?

gracely answered snotty roof

I was under vary attack......

I said laughingly dear! "Beauty" scare herself.

5. Poem - Convoy Of Winter Days

I was left alone in a time of past

I was unhappy to find myself in shield room

I was alive alone in awarded corner

I was guarded by dark lights

pirping sound . where I can

raining in a count..

dancing in a crown..

bleeding in a brown..

wearing in a round..

swearing in a sound..

lowering in a loud..

passing in a shout..

understanding my virtues in a dark time

I was rude to show my beauty tears

but tears realise everything.......

I started blooming

I started considering myself as greif

my organ started sensing as theif

I am stolen in mood

to revolve me in chile time

next door to stanza bar

I believe monsoon was rude that day

sun strikes as dark day

nature has stolen its beauty

no one attacked me , specially caring eminents

next time "beauty shines ˣ

ˣ*monsoon cries*ˣ

no one was attacked in elevation bar

ˣ*Winter* ˣ *quite alone*

hast awake ˣ*beauty trial*ˣ

"Winter" smiled and said

It's my 'TIME'!!

....

6. Poem - Allegedly Convicted Victim

I am convicted to convert sea

into beautiful rivers

I am alleged who forcefully do

BUT...............

I am not liar towards "NATURE"

notorious flower to bushy trees

always laugh on me........

I am innocent creator

I am claiming my own creature

I really want to craft you .....

believe me bushy trees ,

notorious flowers

I am "NATURE"

I am "TRUTH"

I destined this " UNIVERSE "

my creativity , my universe

I need "LOVE"

I need " SHINE"

please don't ignore me

I am bless with you

I am in love with you.......

....

7. Poem - Granting A Gesture

Finding my beam for better

cuddling my life in gesture

what a great day !

Naughty "SUN" to Bushy "CLOUDS"

granting gesture for better

I was frighted with days night

starring someone for cure

prevention is at her "BEAM"

life revelation is her future

many tactics and ways failed

for great granting day,

deeply grilled in frail

but I wasn't "Naive"

that's my gesture...

I welcomed her every penny of seconds..

I wasn't cool enough to speak

for better...............

yet, creating a gesture in smiling face

granting my soul

in dull cool eve..

I was depressed in night hours,

hoping for better charm

gesture approved me....

granting surpasses me ....

I lived , I breathed..

I walked, I smiled...

AND...

Everybody "Shocked"

....

Joy With Star'd Poet's Message

HELLO!

I am nervous until unsure

about truly soul heart......

I believe you got a relief from my Poetry

trying for more better

more improvement in me .

yet , blanket didn't reach face

burried underground.

start leavining in poetry

find your creulity

smiled in difficulty

live in purity

THANKYOU "LEGENDS" for evolving in me

THANKYOU

....

..